Danger Cave

Nino Balistreri

Copyright © Nino Balistreri 2018
Balistrerinino338@gmail.com

Fiction

Design: DnA Design House
Cover: DnA Design House

National Library of Canada Cataloguing in Publication
Caruso, Anthony 1944-
Danger Cave / Nino Balistreri
ISBN: 978-1-7750849-1-4
    I.   Fiction – Adventure

Danger Cave

1 WHO WANTS TO GO?

Trevor Carson slowly crawled through Boston's rush hour traffic, winding his way out of the downtown, where he worked in Management consulting. It was a typical Friday afternoon. The northbound lanes of the expressway were bursting with traffic.

But this Friday, Trevor's home commute was special. His mind was already miles away, thinking of the vacation trip, that will start early tomorrow morning. A mental list was running through his head, of the chores he still had to accomplish.

He was so deep in thought, he almost missed his exit into the subdivision. Thinking, 'Tricia and the kids will be busy packing for the trip'.

Arriving home, he backed the van into the driveway, in order to make loading easier. Reaching for the kitchen door, Trevor opened it carefully, so as not to bang into luggage. The door swung freely. It was clearly evident, there was no luggage in the vestibule.

Turning the corner into the kitchen, he found his wife Tricia sitting at the kitchen table, drinking a mug of tea. She had that 'I could scream look' on her face.

Trevor took a mug from the cupboard and poured himself some hot tea from the Brown Betty pot. Joining Tricia at the table he asked, "Well?" Tricia replied, "Kids! I give up. You deal with them!"

Trevor exited the kitchen and went up the stairs towards the kids bedrooms. In the first bedroom, Trevor found his ten year old son. Xavier was sitting on the floor, playing with his tablet. There was an open duffel bag lying empty on his bed. Trevor sat on the floor next to his son and asked, "What's the problem." Xavier launched into a great dialogue about his confrontation with his mother, "She will not allow me to pack several bags. I need to bring all my favourite toys. And worse still, mom says I am not allowed to bring my ant farm."

Xavier was sure that his dad would side with him, "I know that you understand, so I didn't do any packing." Trevor assured Xavier, "I do understand your need to bring toys. But contrary to your wishes, I must re-affirm your Mother's decree. You pack only your summer and camping clothes. Don't forget your bathing suits, snorkel and fins." He also confirmed Tricia's One Bag Only rule, "We don't want to be crowded with luggage, in the van." Trevor assured Xavier, "There will be lots to do and play with on our holiday trip, trust me." Xavier was not convinced. But knew from experience when he was outnumbered and outranked.

Trevor then left Xavier and proceeded further down the hall to his twelve year old daughters' room. Taped firmly on the closed door was a sheet of paper, stating in bold red marker, VICTORIA'S ROOM KEEP OUT! Trevor knocked on the door. Hearing no response, he slowly opened it and entered. Victoria was sitting on her bed reading a teen magazine.

Trevor sat on her chair and asked, "Is your magazine interesting? Victoria blurted out, "I'm not going! I will stay with Aunt Geri, that way I won't miss my guitar lessons."

Being a patient dad, he calmly explained for what seemed like the tenth time, that all was arranged. "Your guitar teacher gave you pages of daily exercises, after all it is only for two weeks and summer vacation time." He reminded Victoria, "Lots of the kids taking guitar take time off in the summer, to go on vacation and do not fall behind in lessons."

Trevor assured Victoria that she should not worry and to start packing. Emphasizing, "I need your bag tonight in order to load. That way we can get an early start in the morning."

Returning to the kitchen, where Tricia was taking a casserole out of the oven. He looked at her and shrugged, "I think that I put all of the fires out, time will tell." Trevor proceeded to set the table, to help Tricia get ready for the meal.

When it all was completed, he called the kids to come and eat. They both straggled into the kitchen dragging their feet.

It was a quiet meal, devoid of all the usual chatter. Victoria and Xavier had looks on their faces, as if they were heading to a funeral, not a vacation.

Both Trevor and Tricia still had a lot to do. They were too tired to press the kids issues any further. Believing that moods would lighten once they were on the road.

Later that evening Victoria grudgingly dragged her duffel bag to the kitchen door. Returning instantly from her room, she perched her guitar case gingerly against the bag.

Shortly after, Xavier trundled down the stairs dragging his duffel bag. He set it down beside Victoria's. Realizing that Victoria's guitar was sitting there, he suddenly took off running towards his room. In just a few minutes he returned lugging a soft vinyl case that Trevor knew, held his electronic drum set.

It did have a battery back up for power.

Seeing it resting by Victoria's Guitar, Trevor decided that this would have to be acceptable, although possibly not appropriate for camping. Trevor just glanced at Tricia, raised his eyes and continued with the loading.

The last chore he accomplished before calling it a day, was to maneuver the van to the side of the garage in order to hitch up the camper trailer.

2   ON OUR WAY

The alarm went off at seven AM. Trevor did love to get going early. Tricia was already up. She came into the bedroom carrying a mug of coffee for him, "Good luck moving the troops this early."

Trevor took a few sips of coffee then hopped into the shower. It was now seven fifteen. He knocked on both doors and stuck his head in announcing, "If you can be in the van by eight, I will stop at the take out. You can order whatever you want for breakfast." This did the trick. Victoria and Xavier seldom were allowed to order what they liked, as opposed to what was best for them. Heading north on the Interstate, the van was soon clear of the suburbs. Victoria and Xavier were busy in the back seat, devouring their breakfast. Having eaten at home, Trevor and Tricia were working on large take out coffees. They soon started to see some open country.

The fast food breakfast had gone a long way towards lifting spirits. But all was still not jovial. Several times along the way both Victoria and Xavier suggested they leave the highway, to follow a sign to something that looked interesting.

Trevor decreed that they could only stop for a quick lunch, as he had special plans for later that day. Trevor and Trisha refused to tell what it was even after repeated pleadings, but assured both kids that they would enjoy it.

Late in the afternoon they left the main highway. The local road wound eastward towards the sea shore. Xavier spotted a highway sign. It had in bold lettering, 'To International Ferry Terminal'.

Out of curiosity, Xavier and Victoria watched forward to see where their dad was taking them. They both got very excited when after turning a corner, Trevor drove into a parking lot next to a large ship. It was a strange looking thing.

Xavier asked his dad, "Why does it look like two boats underneath?" Trevor explained to Xavier and Victoria, "This type of boat is called a Catamaran. It is basically like the little sailboat that Poppa T has at his cottage. Two hulls connected by a deck. Only this one is powered by two jet engines. Because of this, it goes really fast."

He then announced, "We will be taking the car onto the ship and spending the night at sea, in order to get to the real start of our holiday trip."

Victoria and Xavier were really excited now! Having been on lots of small boats, but never a ship, let alone to sleep overnight.

One by one, the cars like in a parade, slowly wound up the long ramp and into the yawning mouth of the ship. Xavier announced, "It feels like we are Jonah being swallowed by the whale." Everyone laughed at this.

Once inside the ship, there were crew members in bright orange jump suits. They were guided along a narrow marked lane, in order to park tight to other vehicles. This done, everyone was directed to get out of the van and follow the other travellers up a long flight of stairs, to the public areas of the ship.

Tricia had secretly packed a small bag, with pajamas and toiletries that would be needed for the night. It was very exciting for Xavier and Victoria to walk around the ship and also to see their room. It had a large window overlooking the bow of the ship, plus two sets of bunk beds, making it perfect for everyone. Mom and dad could have the bottom bunks. Victoria and Xavier could have top bunks. This eliminated the competition as to 'Who gets the top'.

Both Victoria and Xavier were amazed when they saw their bathroom. It was quite small. It had a tiny stainless steel sink, plus a strange toilet that had a foot pedal and no water tank. The really amazing thing about the bathroom was that in one corner a shower head stuck out of the wall, with taps below it and a floor drain. There was no ledge walls or curtain. Xavier and Victoria had never seen a bathroom like this before.

Once they were settled in their room, everyone went to the restaurant for supper. On the way there they could feel the ship easing away from the terminal. By the time they reached their restaurant booth, through the window there was an awesome scene unfolding. The ship was ever so slowly manoeuvring out of the harbour, towards the open ocean.

Xavier and Victoria were amazed that there could be such a large restaurant on a boat. After supper a movie ran in one of the lounges. Trisha told the kids that this was called a travelog. It showed scenes of the ocean beaches and points of interest where they would be landing.

The following morning after breakfast in the restaurant, everyone went out on deck to look at the approaching land. The ferry rounded a high headland. It had an enormous lighthouse perched on the top edge of the cliff.

They then passed through a narrow channel. The ship started to slow down as it gently glided through the harbour. It then eased up to the dock at a large terminal, similar to the one where they had boarded the ferry. On nearing the terminal the entire bow section began to lift, in order to expose the car decks.

3 ARRIVAL

Shortly, the speakers announced, "All passengers should now return to your vehicles in preparation to disembark." Tricia led Victoria and Xavier down the long stairs to the car deck. Trevor made a detour to their cabin to collect the packed overnight bag.

Once a crew member signalled their van to roll forward, Xavier and Victoria thought that they would just drive off the ship and keep going. To their surprise they had to wait in turn, for a man in a uniform to come and talk to them.

Trevor explained that they were now in Canada and being in a foreign country they had to clear customs. 'Clearing customs' was certainly a new term that Xavier and Victoria had never heard before.

The man in uniform, who Trevor called a Customs Agent, soon came to their car window. He asked Trevor where they lived and if they were American citizens. He also wanted to know how long they intended to stay in Canada.

The last question surprised both Victoria and Xavier! He wanted to know if they were carrying firearms or ammunition. Satisfied with Trevor's answers he announced, "Welcome to Canada, enjoy your vacation."

Driving through the town near the ferry, neither Xavier nor Victoria could see much difference. This town looked like the seaside towns near their home end of the ferry ride. It had the same types of streets and identical big box stores.

Trevor assured them, "We will soon be away from this area. You will see some interesting scenery up ahead. From there the van wound its way out into the country, following a sign that was boldly marked, 'Historic Lighthouse Route'.

4   FISHING PORTS

As they drove along the shore route, the van passed
through several small villages. Each one had a wharf filled
with moored fishing boats. The boats were certainly
interesting. They were all brightly painted in multiple colours.
On closer inspection, everyone chuckled at reading some of
the funny names that fishermen called their boats.

By mid-afternoon they veered off the shore road and
pulled up to a camp ground gate. The sign read, 'Island Park
Provincial Campground'. Trisha explained, "In Canada, they
call the divided areas of the country Provinces, instead of
States."

Trevor went into the office and registered, then they drove to their assigned camping site. After unhooking the camper and setting it up, Trisha suggested that they explore the town. It was visible across the harbour from the camp.

At first it looked like any other small town. But then part way along the main street they turned right and drove one block down. This street followed along the shore.

It was a lot more interesting. First they saw an old cooperage, where they could watch the workers making wooden barrels, the same way that everyone had made them hundreds of years ago. Further along there was a Dory Shop and museum.

On entering the Dory Shop, a man called 'The Dory Maker' explained how dory's were built and how they were used by fishermen years ago, to make their living.

When the Dory Maker finished his talk, they sat on benches and watched a video. It showed old footage, of how the dory's went way out to sea. Each one working from a schooner. Two men in each dory, fished alone in rough water and fog.

The video went on to explain how some times the fog would be so thick, the dory men could not find their way back to the mother ship. When this happened, they never panicked.

They just rowed home, even though it would often take two or more days of hard rowing. Xavier exclaimed that he thought this was great. Victoria made her opinion quite clear, "No way would I ever go out there and do that".

They then wandered further along the historic waterfront. Admiring the many yachts, moored at the Yacht Club. Talking to a yacht-er there, Trevor got directions to a good place to have a seafood supper.

The seafood was great. They ate at a picnic table, beside the small fish market and take out restaurant. As recommended everyone ordered a hot lobster roll with fries. They all loved lobster and had never had it this delicious way.

Following supper it was time to return to the camp ground. The gate attendant told them on passing through, what was happening that evening.

He suggested that if the kids liked to climb, there was an old granite quarry on part of the grounds, plus there would be a movie in the rec hall at dusk. All four took in both activities. Everyone later settled down in the camper for a welcome sleep.

5   UP THE SHORE

The following morning right after breakfast, Victoria and Xavier were in for a surprise. Their dad announced, "It is time to pack up and fold the camper." They had both assumed that this campground was their vacation destination.

Trevor announced, "The campground where we will stay for the next week or so, is up the shore." Seeing the disappointment on their faces, he assured them that the drive there would only take part of the day. "The camp ground where we are heading is near a famous island that as legend says, has Captain Kidd's treasure buried on it." Xavier s eyes went wide at this statement. He had read a story about Captain Kidd and other pirates, in a book that he borrowed from the library.

Trevor drove slowly up the picturesque shore road, stopping in several small fishing villages. They all looked similar to Victoria and Xavier. Getting bored, they started asking, "Are we there yet".

Finally Trevor pulled off the shore road at a sign marked 'Sea Cave Camping Park'. Xavier asked, "What is a sea cave? Do we have to camp in them?" Trevor explained, "I read on line that the campground is not in but beside a grouping of natural caves. They are in the rock cliffs along this part of the coast."

The campground was on a large grassy plane, up high on a cliff. It had a panoramic view of the ocean. Accompanying his dad, while checking in at the camp office, Xavier asked about swimming in the ocean.

They had often camped on Cape Cod, enjoying the beaches and the surf. The owner of the campground told them, "The ocean is not accessible and very dangerous right where we are. But just nearby, only one mile further up the shore, there is a Provincial Park. It has a nice safe sandy beach, and lifeguards."

The rest of the afternoon was taken up with opening up the camper, settling in and preparations for supper.

That evening the campground showed an outdoor movie. Tricia made some popcorn for a treat to go with it.

It was an old space movie that everyone had seen several times. But as there was no TV or anything else to do, they all watched it before turning in for the night.

Their parents had taken Xavier and Victoria to a Drive In movie the previous year, when on holiday. But this time would be their first experience of watching a movie totally out of doors.

6 DANGER

The next morning after breakfast, Xavier asked if he could explore the camp grounds. Trevor said it was OK, "As long as you stay well away from the cliffs and water."

Tricia and Victoria decided that it was a good time to go to the shower rooms. They should not be busy now. Trevor started to putter with the trailer and to tidy up his supplies in the van.

After showering and dressing, Victoria decided to also have a look around the activity areas. At the pool she dipped her foot in the water. It certainly was not heated like the one at home. From there she made her way to the outer area of the adjoining field, wondering if you could see the shore and caves from there.

Victoria could hear the waves crashing against the rocks, somewhere far below. After a bit she spotted Xavier. He was crouched down on the grass, obviously engrossed in something. Victoria slowly crept up closer, to see what her brother was doing.

Xavier had his magnifying glass. He was trying to start a little pile of twigs and grass on fire, using the sun's rays. Victoria yelled, startling him, causing him to jump up.

She reprimanded him, "Now you're in trouble. Just wait till I tell! Mom told you that you were not allowed to play with that and make fires and dad told you to stay away from the cliffs."

Xavier mad a funny face at Victoria and called her, "Scardycat." He then backed a few steps closer to edge. Suddenly a clump of grass gave way, taking it and Xavier out of sight.

Victoria thought that probably her brother had jumped to a lower spot, to try to scare her. But when she edged forward, she could see that there was no lower spot. The magnifying glass was now resting on a tuft of grass near the edge.

To her shock she could see Xavier. He was now floating many feet below in the raging surf.

Victoria started to scream as she ran towards the camping area. Reaching her parents, she frantically told them that

Xavier had fallen into the ocean. Trevor told Tricia to run to the office for help and call 911. He then ran with Victoria to the spot where Xavier had fallen.

He could see Xavier floating in the surf many feet below, but could not see any sign that he was trying to swim.

Quickly stripping off his jacket and shoes Trevor ran off the cliff, plunging feet first into the raging surf, near his son.

Just as Trevor surfaced, he observed Xavier being swallowed into the mouth of the nearby cave, carried by the tidal surge. He started to swim towards him, but was almost instantly drawn back with the returning water flow.

Trevor realized that if he wanted to reach Xavier, he had to work with the surge. Doing this he soon gained distance. Suddenly nearing the mouth of the cave, the incoming wave thrust him through the opening.

Once inside it took Trevor a few seconds for his eyesight to adjust to the dim light, but soon he spotted Xavier. He was thankfully floating face up. While not swimming, he at least looked awake. Trevor quickly swam to him through the churning water. Xavier grabbed his dad shivering.

All Xavier could say was, "Sorry". Holding tight, Trevor tried to comfort him, "Never mind, I am here and you're going to be safe." Trevor said this while not sure himself. His mind was in shock at what had happened in just the last short minutes. Trevor tread water for a bit while trying to size up the situation. They had now drifted with the flow towards the rear of the cavern.

He decided to try and use the surge in reverse, to get them both out of the cave. After three attempts, he realized it would take more strength than he had left.

He was starting to weaken from the temperature of the cold water. Being a diver Trevor was well versed in the dangers of hypothermia, combined with water. The immediate need was somewhere to rest.

Trevor swam supporting Xavier towards the side of the cave, in order to get away from the heaviest effects of the water flow.

By the time he dragged himself and Xavier up onto a small ledge, he was shivering and totally exhausted. Trevor was sorry that he had shed his jacket. Even wet, the extra layer would have helped to warm Xavier some.

7   THE RESCUE

Meanwhile up top, the police had arrived. A small coast guard launch soon anchored just off shore from the cave entrance. Divers could be seen on board suiting up.

Tricia, Victoria and almost everyone from the campground, were standing on the cliff, watching the drama unfold. The police were making sure that everyone stayed well back, not wanting to have to rescue additional victims.

Soon two divers entered the water and began surface swimming towards the cave entrance. The tide was on the rise, making the surge even more violent. It was evident by their methodical preparations, that the divers knew what they were doing.

This was probably not the first time that they had been called, to rescue people from this rocky shoreline. With each surge of the surf they swept closer to the mouth of the cave.

Just before the surf raged through the opening, they sank below the surface. Doing this allowed them to be swept safely into the cave with the incoming rush of seawater.

Once inside both divers quickly surfaced then swam to one side, so not to get sucked back out with the returning surge. Securing a grip on the caves' rock wall, they quickly scanned the interior of the cave.

As fast as their eyes adjusted to the dim light, they were able to see Trevor and Xavier huddled together on a small ledge. It was located across on the other side of the cave.

Allowing the next surge to run in and out, they used the few slack minutes to quickly swim across to the other side of the cave.

Climbing up onto the ledge, they checked Xavier and Trevor over, to be sure there were no broken bones or severe abrasions.

This done, one of the divers began to draw in a fine cord that was attached to his wet suit. He pulled it in slowly to avoid any snags or breaks.

The cord eventually changed to a heavier one. This turned into a rope as he kept hauling. Then suddenly, popping into the cave there was a large floating parcel. Once it was secured on the ledge, the divers quickly untied it and extracted heavy wraps that they placed around Trevor and Xavier.

There was also an assortment of other gear in the parcel. The diver explained, "These things are the same as the breather vests sailors use, to escape a submarine."

"It is too cold and wet here. We will be unable to safely stay where we are for long. The rising tide would soon fill most of the cave." They had to exit as quickly as possible. The diver demonstrated to Trevor and Xavier how the 'escape lungs' worked. He assured them that they would only need to hold onto the rope, that he would clip to each of them.

"The crew on the boat will do the heavy work. They will draw us out through the surf." Trevor being a licensed sport diver easily understood the instructions.

Xavier was torn between terror and excitement, over all that was happening.

His only other thought was that he was probably in more trouble than he had ever gotten into before, with his crazy ideas.

Once everyone was suited up and attached to the safety line, one of the divers gave several sharp tugs on the rope. He then watched as the slack slowly disappeared.

One of the divers was attached first, then Xavier, Trevor and finally the second diver. One by one they slid from the ledge, into the churning water. Breathing through their mouthpieces, they were slowly drawn towards the cave opening. The divers worked hard treading water while keeping everyone off to one side.

Just as they were drawn near the opening, with no warning one diver grabbed Xavier, the other Trevor and pulled them underwater.

The next thing they knew, they were being pulled quickly with the outward surge into the welcoming daylight.

Once well clear of the rock opening, both divers let go of their charges. All four immediately floated to the surface. Above the roar of the surf, both Trevor and Xavier could hear shouting and clapping.

Neither knew what this meant. What they could not see from the level of the surf, was the entire entourage up on the cliff, cheering and clapping. Everyone relieved at seeing four heads, reappear from the depths of the cave.

The boat crew, spotting them bobbing in the waves, began to pull hard and steady, drawing all four seaward towards the rescue launch.

In what seemed like no time, Trevor and Xavier were being lifted into the launch then rushed below decks to a warm cabin. They were stripped of their wet cold clothes and wrapped in heated blankets. Nothing had ever felt better.

The crew hauled anchor and motored up the shore to the nearest marina. Paramedics and an ambulance were waiting on the wharf. Trevor assured them that he felt they were OK. The

Coast Guard divers told him that it was regulations. They had to be examined by a doctor.

At the marina wharf, Trevor and Xavier were made to lie on stretchers and wrapped again in another layer of blankets, then carried off the boat. The ambulance rushed them to the nearby village hospital. When they arrived at the emergency entrance, Tricia and Victoria were anxiously waiting.

Trevor assured them that they were OK. They were immediately whisked into the emergency department. A doctor took their vital signs, and checked them again from head to foot, for injuries.

By now they had finally stopped shivering and were given permission to leave. The doctor warned Trevor, "You must stay nearby for twenty-four hours. It is a precaution in case there are any difficulties arising from your harrowing experience."

Tricia had thankfully brought dry clothes for them. She drove everyone back to the campground.

On arrival, Tricia refused to hear arguments. She immediately settled Trevor and Xavier in chairs to rest, snugly rapped in sleeping bags.

The doctor had told Tricia, to be sure to keep them well warmed for the next twelve hours, to prevent after effects, from their immersion in the cold sea water. After a hot supper they went to bed early, both totally exhausted from the days exertion and excitement.

8   NIGHTMARES

That night Xavier slept soundly, but Trevor was restless. Each time he dozed off, he dreamt of surf water and caves. But strangely at the end of each short dream, of stone steps.

The next morning, Trevor looked as tired as when he had gone to bed. Tricia asked if he was alright, "I think that you may need to see the doctor again?"

Trevor reassured her that he was OK, "I just had a bad night, with strange dreams." Tricia assured him, "It is no wonder you had strange dreams, after what you have been through."

All that day Trevor mused about his dreams. The more he thought about it, the more the strange things he envisioned became reality in his minds eye.

Xavier was careful to stay close to the camp site, afraid to get into any further trouble. He was still wondering if the police would show up to arrest him, or something.

After lunch, Tricia feeling that all was now stable with her world, took Victoria and Xavier on a marked nature walk down the shore.

Once they were away, Trevor walked back across the field to the scene of the accident. He sat on the grass ledge, looking down at the cave entrance. Something was bothering him. He could not get it out of his mind.

After a while he got up and walked over to the camp office. He asked, "Has anyone ever dove purposely into that cave?" The camp owner told him, "According to local stories. Sport divers tried to explore some of the many sea caves, a long time ago. I am not sure which ones. What I am sure of, is that other than at slack low tide, the surge is too dangerous to be safe."

He confirmed, "Diving the caves is not illegal. But it is strongly discouraged. I have heard stories of people being badly hurt. They get flung against the rocks by the current and tidal surge."

9   A FRIEND IN NEED

The following morning after breakfast, Trevor wandered purposely away from the campsite. He did not want Tricia to overhear him making a call. He called his best friend in Boston, Derek Marlie, who was also his dive buddy.

After explaining all that happened, Derek agreed to drive up with his family for a few days camping. He also agreed to bring his boat and both sets of dive gear.

Trevor said nothing to Tricia that day, deciding to wait until Derek arrived.

Then it would be too late for her to talk him out of his scheme. Two days later a familiar SUV pulled up beeping its horn.

Everyone except Trevor was amazed, when Derek Marlie, his wife Geri their son Daniel and daughter Meagan piled out.

After all the greetings, Tricia gave Trevor a stare with that, 'What are you up to look?'

The rest of the afternoon was taken up helping their friends set up camp. After supper Trevor and Derek finally had a chance to wander off together.

They walked over to the cliff and sat on the grass for a while. Tricia assumed that Trevor was telling Derek about the accident. In true fact they were making plans, to dive on the cave to explore.

Instead of a camper, Derek had brought along a large four room tent and his seaworthy Boston Whaler boat.

This would be needed to gain access to the cave entrance. Trevor planned to employ the same method that the Coast Guard rescue team had used.

Once plans were set for the next day, Trevor and Derek joined the rest of their families. Everyone went to the camp fire circle, for the evening's entertainment.

Geri knew that Derek had brought his diving gear. She was used to this, as he hauled 'all that gear' everywhere they went. Tricia however did not know that Derek also had Trevor's gear stowed in his boat.

Trevor decided to try and broach the subject casually around the fire circle. He first mentioned that Derek had brought his diving gear.

Tricia replied, "That's OK, too bad you didn't bring yours". What she really meant was, "Thankfully you didn't bring yours. One emergency is enough for a vacation."

Tricia, while being an active athlete herself, had no interest in water or diving. Actually she had always disliked the idea of Trevor being underwater, where he might not be safe.

Trevor waited until they were alone at bedtime, to confess to Tricia. He pleaded to Tricia, "Please Don't be mad at me, because in truth, I asked Derek to also bring my diving gear." Tricia was not at all pleased. She demanded to know, "What other plans have you two cooked up, behind my back."

Tricia sat on the bed totally dumfounded, as Trevor told her, "We intend to explore the sea cave, that Xavier and I were rescued from."

The next morning, there was a heavy chill over the campsite. It had nothing to do with temperature. Tricia was only speaking to the kids.

Victoria and Xavier picked up on it, knowing that this sometimes happened, when their parents had a major disagreement.

Both wondered what it was about. Xavier was sure that it probably had something to do with his accident. What puzzled him was, his mother was talking to him normally. It was just his dad that was getting the silent treatment and extremely cold looks. Trevor clearly was the one that had to be in trouble.

10 EXPLORING

By mid morning Trevor and Derek were busy organizing the boat. Xavier was excited too. He usually went with his dad and Uncle Derek. His job was to stay in the boat as 'lookout', while they dove. This time unhappily, he was told that he would not be able to go.

Upset, Xavier grouched, "Some holiday! I have to stay here while you have all the fun!" Trevor assured Xavier that he will be having fun, "But this dive is just way too dangerous for you to help us by being on the boat."

Xavier wondered what could be too dangerous? He always went with them when they dove on the lakes. All of a sudden, he realized what was happening. He exclaimed, "The cave! You are diving on the cave!"

Trevor confirmed his suspicion, "Yes, that's why you can't come this time. We can't be certain of the surf and how it will bounce the boat around."

"What you can do though to help us, is set up a watch. Keep an eye on the boat from the cliff top. You can signal us with the canned air horn, if the boat looks to be in trouble. We should be able to hear that from inside the cave."

While not as good as being on the boat, Xavier felt that at least he had a part in the adventure. Keeping the boat safe, would be keeping his dad, and uncle safe.

Before long, Derek had the boat trailer hooked to his SUV. He and Trevor drove off, heading up the shore to the nearby marina that offered a launch ramp.

Xavier dragged a lawn chair over, so that he could sit and watch with his dad's binoculars. He settled into the chair, and set the air horn in the drink holder. The entire inlet was in full view as well as the cave openings. Xavier would have liked to be just a bit closer, but surviving one fall off the cliff was a very good lesson for him.

11 STRANGE SIGHTS

Once launched, Trevor and Derek motored the boat south along the shore until they spotted the cliff, with Xavier dutifully sitting on guard above.

Estimating distances at approximately what the coast guard had done. They set two anchors to be extra safe, then started to don their wet suits and diving gear.

Taking a lead from the Coast Guard rescue team, they attached several hundred feet of floating rope to the boat. Derek being the stronger swimmer back flipped into the water first, with the other end of the rope clipped to his dive belt.

He began to swim towards the cave entrance, as Trevor fed the rope out, so as not to have any fowls.

Once it was all floating free with the current, Trevor back flipped into the water, then stroked towards Derek. On reaching him, they observed the cave entrance for a few minutes, in order to monitor the rhythm of the wave surge.

By using it to their advantage, they could safely slide underwater and ride the surge all the way in. Trevor reminded Derek, "Once we surface in the cave, we need to swim instantly to the right, to get away from the returning surge. This would put us at the base of the ledge where Xavier and I took refuge."

Following Trevor's plan, he and Derek swam nearer to the cave entrance. The closer they got, the more the surge pulled and pushed them.

About twenty feet before reaching the cave entrance, Trevor slid beneath the waves and Derek followed.

At this point it was just a matter of staying at a stable depth, allowing the surge to carry them through the cave opening.

Once inside they surfaced and quickly swam over to the ledge. There was no time to waste in lifting themselves clear of the water, to ensure that the ebb flow did not grab them.

Their first task was to check the waterproof lights and equipment for damage. All looked in good shape. They proceeded to remove their tanks and fins, securing them well up on the ledge.

Turning the torches on, Trevor and Derek looked around to see what lay above. True to Trevor's dream, there were rough steps hew n out of the rock.

Following up a ways, the steps branched out in two directions, both leading to dead ends. Everything was wet, and covered with sea slime.

Half way back down, a flash caught Trevor's eye. His torch had wavered sideways. The beam of light reflected off something that was embedded in the rock wall.

On closer examination Trevor could see that it was a piece of old glass. Rubbing it clean did not result in any further discovery. He showed it to Derek. They began to slowly examine the walls on both sides of the stairway.

Working their way up and down both staircases, they found several more pieces of embedded glass, on each side. Aiming their lanterns individually on each one, did not expose any startling revelations.

Once back down to the ledge, it was evident that the tide was surging dangerously higher.

Trevor observed out loud, "Something seems strange to me. Even though the cave entrance is now totally submerged, I still have a slight feeling of a fresh moving air current. I had expected the air in this cave to be somewhat stale and dank." They shone their torches all around, but could not readily see any other openings or obvious sources of air.

Freeing the rope end from the rocks, the next process was to reverse their swim back to the boat It was imperative to accomplish this before the tidal surge rose any higher in the cavern. The swim out was a great deal slower.

With no crew member aboard the boat to haul them out. It was necessary to hand haul along the rope. It was only possible to gain distance with each outgoing surge, then holding tight so as to not be swept back. Free swimming was impossible under these conditions.

Once safely aboard Derek's boat, they pulled in the safety rope. It had to be carefully stored, avoiding tangles. This done Trevor hauled both anchors, as Derek started the engine and engaged the shift. They motored back to the marina launch site and loaded the boat, deciding to call it a day.

After supper they sat by the camp fire and discussed their findings with Tricia and Geri. Both Trevor and Derek thinking that more heads would hopefully come up with a reason for the steps and embedded glass. Many theories were discussed, but with no conclusions.

12 AN IDEA

By mid-morning the following day, Trevor and Derek were sitting with coffee, once again trying to make sense of what they had seen.

Shortly, Victoria came running from the outer field clearly agitated. She blurted out, "Xavier is at it again!" When asked, "At what?", she stated, "It is the same as the other day. Xavier was trying to start a fire with his magnifying glass. That's how he fell off the cliff. He was trying to get away from me, so he would not get in trouble."

Trevor just shook his head and stood up, to walk over and see what Xavier was up to now.

Derek followed out of curiosity. What they found was Xavier and Daniel, crouched down in the field. This time thankfully, well back from the cliff.

They had gathered a small pile of grass and twigs. Xavier was angling the sun through his magnifying glass, trying to set it all alight. Being so engrossed in what they were doing, they were not aware of their fathers' approach.

Trevor exclaimed, "Xavier!" and both boys jumped to their feet in the process dropping the magnifying glass. After a scolding about fires and safety, Trevor picked the glass up and sent both boys off, back to the campsite.

Standing beside Derek looking out to sea, Trevor suddenly realized that he was holding the magnifying glass out. He could clearly see that it was throwing a steady beam downward towards the ground. He pointed to it in amazement exclaiming, "Look!"

Derek looked wide eyed at the beam of light. Both their eyes lit up at the same time. There were so many pieces of glass embedded in the walls, it had to be for reflection. It would mean another expedition to the cave, to examine it closely. This time actually know knowing what to look for.

Luckily Tricia and Geri had taken Victoria with them to town for a grocery run. This saved them from announcing their intentions. Giving Xavier and Daniel the chore, of once again keeping watch from the cliff. They quickly hitched the boat to the SUV, got all their gear in order, then headed up the shore.

The tide was low, but it all too soon would be on the rise. They had no time to waste.

Quickly launching the boat from the marina, they repeated their journey south along the shore, to the cave entrance inlet, where they carefully set the two anchors.

Both were very excited, but still did not cut corners when it came to safety. Being well schooled divers, they knew that cutting corners invited disaster.

They attached the guide rope, and went through their check of all the needed safety equipment. Paying special attention to the high powered torches. Without them properly operating, the dive would be a wasted effort.

As quickly as possible, yesterdays' process was repeated. Drifting rope, then approaching the cave entrance. The wave and surge action was slightly less today. Plus having completed an ingress and digress of the cave before, helped them to gain entrance easily.

Climbing upon the ledge, they unpacked their torches and immediately started scanning the cave ceiling instead of the walls. At first it looked like there was nothing to see.

Slowly though, as their eyes adjusted to the gloom, they honed in, absorbing more detail. They observed that the cave roof certainly rose steadily to a high point. And sure enough there it was!

Approximately fifty feet back from the cave entrance, just around where the ceiling naturally peaked. Instead of just solid rock there was a large clump of roots, with bits of light shining through.

Both Trevor and Derek studied it for a while, to try and get a fix as to where it lay in distance, back from the cave entrance. The unknown factor being the thickness of the rock at the channel entrance. Feeling satisfied that they had calculated the positioning as close as possible, it was time to strap their tanks on and start the process of exiting the cave.

Safely on board the boat, they motored back to the marina, while anxiously discussing their findings. They could hardly wait to load the boat and rush back to the campground.

13 THE SEARCH

On the way back, Derek detoured to the nearby town of Lunenburg. It was located on a famous harbour. The worlds fastest schooner of its day, 'The Bluenose' had been built there.

Parking at the hardware supply, to purchase two hundred feet of light but sturdy rope, and a large pry bar, plus a sharp edged folding shovel.

Arriving at the campground, they let Xavier and Daniel go off to play, then proceeded over to the field above the cave. Derek being the hyper organizer had suggested staking and stringing out a grid pattern in the field.

Trevor convinced him that doing it this way, would draw too much attention to their activities.

Instead, after pacing approximately the distance they had estimated back from the cliffs edge, Derek used a rock to pound a sturdy stake into the grass. This was to create a center point to work from.

Tying a loop on one end of the rope, he slipped it over the stake. They started working in an ever widening circle, taking turns poking the ground every foot or two with the large crow bar. Both believed that they were just feet away from the grown over soft spot.

After almost an hour, the circle had widened quite a bit. It was now appearing too close and too far from the cliff edge. They decided to slowly re trace their probing, agreeing that they had probably overstepped the magic spot.

Sure enough, about half way back and off to the left the crow bar easily sank, deeper than it had at any other point.

Trevor started to pry around that spot, while Derek went back to their camp site to get the shovel. By the time he returned, Trevor was aggressively thrusting the crow bar deep into the ground. After digging almost two feet through old sod and roots, the hole in the rock cavern was exposed.

Trying to determine the position of the ledge, and steps, in relation to the cliff, they then graded the earth around the opposite side of the opening so that when the sun passed over at mid-day tomorrow, it hopefully will shine easily through the opening, at the right angle.

The present position of the sun, told them that this day was too far gone.

The sun was now too low in the horizon, to reflect its rays at the right angle, to penetrate the opening. It would be mid-day tomorrow before the sun will be high enough for it to possibly beam through the hole, and onto the glass reflectors in the cave.

Trevor dragged an old dead branch over and set it above the opening. It would not do if a camper out for an evening stroll broke a leg stumbling into it, even if the hole was too small to fall through.

They returned to the camp ground and joined their families for supper and the evening's activities. Both were bubbling with excitement wondering what tomorrow would bring. Every once in a while their eyes would meet and they would smile broadly at each other.

At one point Tricia saw this. She could tell that they were up to something. She was already upset, because they had sneaked off, to dive the cave again today.

Also observing what was going on, Geri confronted them, "What are you two cooking up now? Tricia and I can tell by

the expressions on your faces that you are up to something?"
They both just shrugged and let on that nothing was up.
Till they could learn more about the meaning of the steps and
the glass, what else could they say?

14 SEARCHING THE PAST

The following morning, both Trevor and Derek had difficulty working their way through breakfast without showing their excitement. By mid-morning they told Tricia and Geri that they had decided to visit the cave, "Just one more time".

Neither wife was pleased about this and reminded them that it was also 'their' vacation. Insisting that the husbands had better soon start participating in activities with them and the kids.

Trevor and Derek promised both, "After this dive, we will for sure be more attentive and participate in everything.

While Derek was hitching the boat trailer to his van, Trevor walked over to the field. Once there, he removed the branch that was covering the now excavated hole.

On the way to the marina, a stop was made at the builders supply. This time to purchase a hammer stone chisel small crow bar and extra waterproof batteries for their torches.

Spotting the cleaning products isle, Trevor grabbed a spray bottle of bathroom cleaner and a package of coarse scrub pads.

Arriving at the marina, they quickly launched the boat then proceeded to motor down the shore to their now familiar anchorage spot. Following the same procedure, soon saw them standing on the ledge inside the cave.

After shedding their dive gear. The next chore was to use the scrub pads to clean the slime from all of the glasses that were embedded along the side walls of the stairs.

Completing this, they then sat down on the ledge near the base of the steps, facing the now brightly shining opening, in the cavern roof. A steady shaft of weak light glowed, now that the roots and sod had been cleared away.

It was just a matter of time, to wait till the sun rose to mid-day height. As twelve noon approached they both stood, being careful not to block any of the glass insets.

Sure enough! Just as their watches hit twelve, the sun's rays shone through the opening. At first nothing happened, but then after a few minutes, the ray strengthened and hit one of the lower glasses. What they had not realized before, was that every piece of glass had a reflective substance, imbedded behind it.

In just a few seconds, it was evident that the suns reflection was now hitting a corresponding glass, on the opposite side of the stairs, just a little further up. Second by second as the sun's rays strengthened, the beam of light carried further on up the stairs, from side to side, glass to glass.

Trevor and Derek belly crawled up the steps following the ever travelling beam, being careful not to interfere with its progress. Strangely at the split in the staircase, it continued only up the left branch.

This confirmed their theory, that one or other of the branches in the passage, had to be a decoy. Reaching the top, the beam of light shone directly on the rock face, not glass. They looked at each other as much as to ask, 'what does this mean'?

Now knowing where the sun beam ended, they headed back down the steps to retrieve their torches and tools.

15 DISCOVERY

Back at the top, Trevor and Derek examined the rock face closely, using their torches. In poor light it had looked the same as the other ending, like a solid rock face. In bright light, it actually turned out to be carefully mortared together slabs of flat rock.

The sealed opening was a bit over four feet high, and three feet wide. Seeing a tiny crack near the bottom Derek hammered the small crow bar in. Once he had a good grab he levered it. Nothing moved. He then worked his way all around the slab. Still no movement!

Meanwhile Trevor was carefully running his torch beam along the mortared seams, while feeling with his fingers. He was working slowly in an upward motion, over the entire rock face. The pattern in the pieces finally led him to a small section at the top. It was barely a foot square.

Trevor pointed this out to Derek, "This small piece looks to be set slightly different. Could it be like the key block at the top of a Roman arch?" Derek proceeded to chip away at the small slab. Sure enough, this piece had been the key to the stone work! It soon came free, allowing them to easily dismantle the rest of the wall.

Once it was all cleared away, they shone both torches into the opening. Both were wide eyed, as the torches revealed what lay behind the rock wall. There stood an old hand hew n, iron bound wooden door. It was secured with a large old fashioned rusted iron padlock.

16 PIRATES

The wood was badly deteriorated. It took little effort to pry the lock and hasp from the door frame. Swinging the door open was another matter. The rusty hinges made it difficult.

Trevor and Derek used every ounce of their strength, prying and pulling. Finally after a long while, they were able to get the door ajar just enough to squeeze through.

Once inside, their torches lit up a small room. It was more like a mini cave. Grouped before them, nestled on the sandy floor, were several iron bound wood boxes and small chests.

Trevor exclaimed, "Oh great! After all this effort, we have probably found an old rum runner's stash."

Derek replied, "I don't think so. Rum would not be in chests, or iron bound boxes. Rum bottles would be in open wood boxes, or bulk in kegs.

Both Trevor and Derek's hearts were now racing. What had they found? They closely examined each iron bound box and chest. They all appeared to be well sealed. Trying to slightly lift each, it was obvious. All of them were either waterlogged or heavy with contents.

No amount of effort would allow them to be even slightly shifted. Trevor decided out loud, "I can't stand it, I have to open one now!"

Derek held his torch on the nearest chest, while Trevor slid the small pry bar in behind the hasp and lock. Being careful to not do any more damage than necessary, Trevor eased the hasp away from the wood.

He then stood up joining Derek in a trance like state, staring at the still closed chest.

Gathering his nerve, Trevor knelt back down. He tried to lift the lid. It was rusted to the metal straps. He took the small pry bar and slid it under the front edge. Then wedging the front corners in turn, he slowly eased the lid up as Derek shone his torch fully on it.

As fast as the lid swung back Trevor stood in shock!

Neither he nor Derek could move or say a word. Could it be real? Or were they both hallucinating? The chest was filled to the brim with what looked like, Spanish gold doubloons!

After what seemed like forever, Trevor and Derek both knelt down as if in homage, to look closer. They were not dreaming! Before them was a chest of gold coins. They were unevenly shaped and stamped with various strange designs. Trevor and Derek reached out and picked up several coins to get a closer look. They were obviously very old.

Derek looked at Trevor, "If this chest is filled with gold coins, what is in the others?" They moved to the next, a small wooden crate. This time Trevor held the torch, and Derek went to work easing the boards away from the top.

They were old and rotten. Even though Derek was careful, most of them crumbled at the edges.

Once the boards were cleared, there was a piece of heavy cloth covering the contents. It looked like a chunk of old frayed sail. Derek lifted it away and once again they both stared in shock.

The crate was neatly laid with rows of what looked like gold bars. The bars were about ten to twelve inches long and two to three inches thick. Uneven in texture, rounded at the ends and sides. Each one looked similar to an oversized candy bar roll. Derek picked one up and was amazed by its weight. Looking it over he observed several strange letters and markings.

Next in line was another small chest. Repeating the process Trevor worked the lid free, assuming that he would find more coins. To his surprise and shock, it was filled with beautiful pearls of white pink and even some large smokey black ones.

Totally amazed, Derek and Trevor took turns opening crates and chests. In several there were more coins.

Two of the smaller chests were filled with the most incredible gold and silver jewelry. Each piece heavily encrusted with gems of many colours. The two largest of the wood crates were filled with ornate gold plates and goblets.

Derek was the first to say anything since the opening of the crates and chests began. Picking up a gold plate, "Well I think that Geri can now forget about coveting that ironstone dish set, that the kitchen store has on sale." They looked at each other and laughed, finally breathing easier for the first time in over an hour.

17 PLANS

Once Derek and Trevor's heartbeat and breathing returned to normal. It was decided that if they were back at the campground and away from all the treasure, they would be able to think clearer. Decisions had to be made, on what to do next.

Each had a divers pouch attached to their knife belts. It took a few minutes to select a sampling of the smaller pieces from the chests.

They then exited the cave, using the now familiar rope process. Neither spoke at all about the cave or its contents, through t the trip back to the marina, or on the drive to the campground.

Arriving at the camp, Trevor could see that his Van was gone. In Derek's tent there was a note on the bed, stating that

Tricia Geri and the kids being tired of waiting for 'the boys' to return, decided to drive up the shore to see some of the local sites.

Once Derek had the boat unhitched, he put on a pot of tea. Meanwhile Trevor returned to the field and secured the dead branch back over the excavated hole.

While the tea was steeping, 'the boys' went to the shower room to wash off the salt, It was now uncomfortably dried on their skin. Clean and dressed in dry clothes, they sat down on camp chairs under the camper awning, to try and formulate what their next move would be.

Both realized that even though they found the treasure, there would ultimately be a legal question of ownership.

Trevor believed that the ownership of the cave would be an important factor. Mulling around several ideas and plans. Both agreed that the treasure was too massive and heavy to even think of sneaking it all away. As tempting as that would be.

Finally, they realized that they were talking in circles, with no real idea of how to proceed. Trevor suggested that he call a friend of his in Boston, who practised marine and international law.

A lengthy call to Trevor's friend, James Gordon. Filling him in on all that had transpired, in the end gave them at least an interim plan to proceed by.

Trevor promised James that he would call back in the next day or two, to bring him up to date on how they were progressing, given his instructions.

James got very excited talking about the treasure. He offered to head their way the next day. Trevor assured him that there was no rush. It would be better if he came up later, once he had thoroughly researched their legal position.

18 CONFESSIONS

Later in the afternoon the van rolled in, discharging Geri Tricia and the kids. There was the usual commotion, followed by the unpacking of groceries and preparation for supper. The plans for that evening included another outdoor movie.

Derek suggested that the kids go together, so the adults could stay back at the camp site. All four kids wondered about this. Any suggestion of freedom always meant, that there was another reason hiding behind it.

Trevor offered to go to the camp canteen to purchase popcorn, chips, chocolate bars and pop.

That did it for sure. All four kids jumped at the chance of a rare evening of junk food. 'Like who cares about parents, or what movie is playing'.

Both Geri and Tricia, watching this exchange wondered what was up. At one point Tricia looked as if she was about to object, but when she glanced at Trevor, he gave her a really strange look and shook his head. Now her curiosity was running overtime.

After supper they all went to the field and played circle Frisbee. Trevor wanted to make sure that he did not get questioned, especially in front of the kids. Preferring the privacy that they would have during the movie.

When dusk finally arrived, they bundled the kids off to the movie with all their treats. Derek appeared with a bottle of wine and four glasses. Trevor lit a small fire in the fire pit on their site. Taking a glass of wine they all sat in a circle.

Trevor looked at Derek hoping that he would start the tale but Derek pointed to him, "You started the adventure, so you start the story. I will help out from where I became involved".

Tricia looked at Geri who was like her shaking her head. Both were just imagining, what trouble their scheming husbands had gotten into this time.

Neither was prepared for the shock of the tale that Trevor started to tell. Derek took over the story at the point in which they broke through the stone wall, in order to expose the cavern.

Both wives were not sure, thinking that possibly the 'boys' were handing them a 'tall tale', to cover up the fact that they had not been around.

In the end though, they could tell by their serious expressions, that amazingly, it had to all be true!

Trevor explained about his call to James Gordon in Boston. He repeated what the lawyer suggested and emphasized that he would need both Tricia and Geri as witnesses, when they talked to the camp owner about the caves.

19 DEALS

Seeing that the lights were still on in the camp office, Trevor wandered over. As casually as he could, he asked the owner Mr. Walters about the adjoining property. Was it public land or part of the campground?

Mr. Walters stated that the field and fifty acres around it was all his property. Trevor then asked if the caves were considered to be his also? He confirmed this, "Yes, it was the caves that originally attracted me to this property".

"I had thought that they could be used as a swim attraction, like the famous Blue Grotto."

"By the time I set up the infrastructure for the campground, I realized that with the unpredictable surf and surging tides, they were probably too dangerous for the public to access."

"On getting legal advice from my agent, I was assured that I could never afford enough insurance, to allow my guests to swim there."

Mr. Walters admitted, "I am aware that you and your friend have been diving in that cave. I said nothing because you approached it from the water rather than from my land. This frees me from any legal liability, if you are injured.

Trevor asked if he could wait a minute because he wanted to tell him something, but he needed his friends help.

Trevor rushed back to the campfire, to collect Tricia Derek and Geri. On the way back he instructed them to follow his lead and not say a word about treasure.

Entering the office, Trevor introduced everyone to Mr. Walters. Trevor then told him, "Derek and I found some old things in the cave, possibly left behind years ago by other explorers and divers."

He suggested, "We would like to bring it all out, but this would cost time and money for compressed air and supplies. We would still like to do it, as long as you agreed to split any worthwhile articles three ways."

Mr. Walters thought that this was an OK deal. "At my senior age, I certainly have no desire to swim underwater, or enter into a dangerous cave."

Tricia asked him for the use of his computer. Soon they had worked out a basic agreement.

Trevor knew that this would not legally serve in the end. The government would probably try to attempt a way to jump in. But at least, according to Trevor's lawyer, James Gordon. It would hold for now.

Tricia printed off several copies, then Trevor, Derek, Tricia, Geri, Mr Walters and also Mrs Walters who had to be fetched from behind the projector, signed and witnessed it.

Trevor asked the Walters if they would kindly come over to the campsite after the movie? To have a glass of wine and see a small sample of 'the stuff' that had been found in the cave.

The Walters reluctantly agreed, "Just for a short visit. It will be late and we want to turn in."

Later when the kids had been tucked into bed, the adults were all settled in chairs around Trevor's campfire. Trevor poured everyone a glass of wine, then went into his camper returning with two small canvas divers pouches.

Trevor asked everyone to hold a hand out.

Then he silently went around the circle dropping several gold Doubloons, silver Reals, three colours of pearls and an assortment of gems into each persons' hand.

No one spoke! They all just stared in total disbelief, at what they were holding. Mr. Walters finally spoke up, "Is this a joke?" He then looked at Trevor and Derek's faces, realizing in shock that they were dead serious.

Trevor and Derek then related the story, as they had with Geri and Tricia. Another round of wine relaxed everyone a bit. Mr. Walters suggested that under the circumstances everyone should call them by their first names, Hazel and Richard.

Trevor related that he would probably hear back from the Boston lawyer, in the next day or so, as to what they legally had to report to authorities.

For the first time, the question was raised as to whose treasure it had been. Richard stated that groups had for many years been actively digging up an island, just north of them. It was following old tales that it held the secret of Blackbeard's treasure. "This area was supposed to have been Blackbeard's stomping grounds."

"Many fortunes and lives, have been lost, searching for his treasure." It was unanimously agreed that such a large stash had to be it. No minor pirate could have gathered such a vast amount of treasure and not be well documented in history, as well as seafaring lore.

20 TREASURE TROVE

The next few days were hectic. Derek Trevor and Richard drove into Halifax. Through Richards' bank they were given the name and location of a reputable security vault company.

Once there, they rented a storage vault, plus made arrangements for the hire of a nondescript armored van. It was arranged to arrive at the campground late every afternoon, to pick up the daily collection of treasure.

Then to the industrial park to shop at a professional marine supply.

They required a large quantity of tanks, ropes, canvas pouches and float bags. Finally to the builders supply for heavy duty plastic bins with lids. Also a shipping strap set up, for sealing the bins.

At the marina, through a friend of Walters', they rented what they called, a Cape Island Boat. It was large enough to safely anchor off the cave entrance.

The idea of winching the treasure up through an enlarged hole in the field, while sounding good, would be too difficult and dangerous to rig. The natural opening was in the centre of the cavern ceiling, directly above the main thrust of the tidal surge. Not to mention that such activity being completely visible, would all too easily attract curiosity seekers.

Tricia Geri Richard and the four kids made up the boat crew. Hazel hated boats. She was happy to stay behind to run the campground.

After being horribly sea sick the first day out, Richard opted to stay ashore, to assist Hazel. Trevor reminded the Walters that in future, running the camp ground could be just a hobby, rather than a necessity, to bolster their meagre retirement pensions.

All went well aboard the boat for three days, but the novelty soon wore off for the kids. Just being anchored in one spot was no fun. A plan was quickly organized where Tricia and Geri took daily turns staying on shore, in order to truck the kids around to various attractions and activities.

Trevor and Derek made three strenuous trips a day in and out of the cave. Transferring treasure in heavy canvas pouches, suspended from float bags.

The Cape Islander was used in the winter months as a lobster boat. It had a marvellous lift pulley system on one side. This machinery was designed to haul heavy strings of lobster traps from the sea floor.

It worked like a charm. Allowing either Geri or Tricia to haul the long line with the canvas bags and floats attached. As they in turn reached the boat, it was strong enough to lift the weight aboard.

Having a power driven line also alleviated the exhausting effort that was needed, to hand haul themselves from the cave. Because of the tides and surf they did not have a lot of time each day, to safely work.

The alternate, to increase their accessibility time, would be to work during the night slack tide, using lights. They decided that this would not only be too dangerous, it would use up strength that they did not have to spare. Also it would run a high risk of attracting unwanted attention to their activities.

Unloading at the marina, they kept as low a profile as possible. Lifting the sealed containers into the bed of Derek's SUV, then transporting them back to the campground. There they met up with the armored van.

Every afternoon although tired from diving, they followed the armored van into Halifax, to supervise the unloading of the cases of treasure, into the secured vault.

Hazel, so happy not to be on the boat and knowing that everyone was busy, kindly cooked some meals. The odd day whoever was out and about with the kids, picked up pizza or other treat food.

James Gordon faxed a great deal of material and legal information, as to how an announcement should be made. He also insisted that they do not contact authorities. He assured Trevor, "The powers to be, will jump in fast, as soon as they get wind of the announcement."

As per James Gordon's advice, they planned to not make the news of the discovery public right away. Not until all of the treasure was safely stored in the vault.

A full week later the transfer was complete. Exhausted, the next step was for Trevor, Tricia, Derek and Geri to notify their employers.

Not fearing for their immediate financial futures, they announced that they had run into difficulties while on holiday.

77

They would need to take an additional week or two off. This was not welcome news for any of the four employers.

21 TELL THE WORLD

It took several days after finishing the transfer of treasure, to begin the next phase of the process. Through a friend in Boston, who was highly internet savvy. They were able to leak a news item on Social Media, 'A pirate treasure has been found on the east coast of Canada. Possibly that of the famous Blackbeard'. They let the buzz run around the news media for three days.

On the second day, Derek and Trevor drove casually past the causeway, to the island where everyone had traditionally dug, searching for the treasure.

The chained off causeway was completely blocked by news media cars and vans. They had obviously jumped to the conclusion that the discovery had been made there. All were hoping to get an early scoop on the breakthrough.

Late afternoon on the third day, an announcement was sent to media sources, 'There will be a press conference to reveal the facts about the treasure. It will take take place at the vault company's facility in Halifax'.

The vault people called in extra security guards, to ensure that only credentialed newspaper and television reporters could gain admittance.

On the day of the announcement, there were several television news vans, resplendent with satellite dishes mounted on their roofs. They were all set up in the parking lot of the vault company's facility.

Tricia, Trevor, Geri, Derek and the four kids, plus Hazel and Richard Walters all parked at the back. They were let quietly in through the employee entrance door.

It took an hour with the help of security staff, to lay open all of the plastic chests, on several long tables. The security company had poles set up with red velvet ropes strung. No one could get close enough to handle, or take samples of.

Portable dividers were strategically placed across the room splitting it in two. This allowed the media people to set up their cameras and sound equipment under supervision.

The guards would insure that no media persons would be able to have an advanced peek at the treasure.

When it all was set and ready, the doors were opened and the reporters were let into the room. A line of guards formed and the dividers were removed. Trevor then Derek related their stories, as the reporters taped and filmed.

That finished, the guards slowly stepped to the sides, to allow the cameras to film the treasure, all the time making sure that no one attempted to go beyond the rope barricade.

That evening the local and national newscasts in both Canada and The United States, all featured footage of the amazing treasure find.

As James Gordon had anticipated. The following day Derek and Trevor were served with a halt order, by the Provincial Courts.

Named as the claimants in the halt order, were both the treasury and heritage sectors of the Province of Nova Scotia. Both departments were hoping to legally gain a claim to the treasure.

An immediate date was set for a hearing. It would take place at the Provincial Court in Halifax, in two days. The Provinces' lawyers were not taking chances that the treasure might be quickly removed from the area.

James Gordon immediately flew in to represent the parties. He was confident that they were on solid ground as far as ownership.

On hearing all the evidence from both sides. The Judge who was well versed in marine law, set down his decision.

"Had Trevor and Derek discovered the treasure beneath the waves in Canadian waters, the government certainly would have grounds for a substantial if not full claim."

Luckily for all concerned, "However the treasure has been found high and dry, on private property."

"Because of this important factor, it is the decision of the courts, that the treasure belongs solely to the property owners and their partners."

The Judge in his summation did however state, "Taking into consideration, the size and scope of the treasure. In the spirit of the judgement, the court would kindly request a sample display of each category of treasure and artifacts to be donated to the Provincial and Maritime Museums of Halifax. In order that it be available for the public to view."

Derek & Trevor certainly felt that it was a more than reasonable request. They asked the judge for a ten minute recess, so that they could confer with their lawyer and partners.

In a private conference room, James Gordon gave his advice. "The judge is a smart man. He knows that you could take all of the treasure completely."

"He also knows that by doing this, it will leave the door open, for the government to launch an appeal. By the simple fact of you agreeing to set aside a portion of treasure for the museums, it makes the likelihood of any appeal being successful, all but impossible.

Returning to the court, James Gordon addressed the judge, "We have all agreed to work with the Curator of Museums, to choose an appropriate group of artifacts, and samples of treasure, that would well represent the find, in a permanent display. They will be given to both the Maritime Museum and the Provincial Museum."

THE END

EPILOGUE

Hazel and Richard Walters had no family. They soon became honorary grandparents to Xavier Victoria Daniel and Meagan.

The Walters' kept running the camp ground during the Nova Scotia summer season. They traded their mobile home for a fine new bungalow on the property, plus a beautiful condo in Florida for the winter months.

They also had the cave roof opening in the field enlarged with a caged steel staircase built. Tourists could now go down safely at low tide times, to explore the stone steps and treasure room.

Waterproof lighting was installed in the cave for safety, as well as a special high intensity needle spot laser. It was strategically aimed at the first glass insert.

When this beam was activated by visitors pressing a button, they were able to experience the directional beam as it climbed the stairs, at any time of the day.

A new office for the camp ground was built. It had an adjoining concrete monitored secure room, in order to exhibit small samples of each type of treasure from Blackbeard's stash. Trevor, Trisha, Derek and Geri all retired from their jobs in Boston. Both couples bought large park model trailers, setting them up permanently at the Walters' campground.

From then on, they spent every summer with the kids. Helping their new friends and partners manage the crowds.

With the additional hiring of local students, they gave guided tours of the pirate cave, through the full summer season.

Danger Cave

ABOUT THE AUTHOR

The author was born in Barrie, Ontario and spent his teenage years in Chicago and North Bay, Ontario. He moved to Toronto where he spent ten years studying and working, particularly in social work. Then it was on to Ottawa where he spent nine years working in chronic care and rehab. In the early 1990's, he moved to Nova Scotia where he managed the office for an arts centre and an MD therapist. Around that time, he started writing seriously and has been doing so ever since.

Danger Cave

OTHER BOOKS BY NINO BALISTRERI

Watch for the next treasure adventure, **'Anchorage of Gold'** by Nino Balistreri set in New England and The Florida Keys.

Also in print a seaside drama involving spies and submarines. **'Death's Secret'** unfolds, in a pristine Nova Scotia port.